KU-594-482

Red Rockets
and
Rainbow Jelly

Sue Heap and Nick Sharratt

PUFFIN

This is Nick.

Red Rockets
and
Rainbow Jelly

For Nick – S.H.

For Sue – N.S.

PUFFIN BOOKS

Published by the Penguin Group
Penguin Books Ltd, 80 Strand, London WC2R 0RL, England
Penguin Group (USA), Inc., 375 Hudson Street, New York, New York 10014, USA
Penguin Books Australia Ltd, 707 Collins Street, Melbourne, Victoria 3008, Australia
Penguin Books Canada Ltd, 10 Alcorn Avenue, Toronto, Ontario, Canada M4V 3B2
Penguin Books India (P) Ltd, 11 Community Centre, Panchsheel Park, New Delhi – 110 017, India
Penguin Group (NZ), cnr Airborne and Rosedale Roads, Albany, Auckland 1310, New Zealand
Penguin Books (South Africa) (Pty) Ltd, Block D, Rosebank Office Park, 181 Jan Smuts Avenue,
Parktown North, Gauteng 2193, South Africa

Penguin Books Ltd, Registered Offices: 80 Strand, London WC2R 0RL, England

puffinbooks.com

First published 2003
Published in this edition 2004
018

Text and illustrations copyright © Sue Heap and Nick Sharratt, 2003
All rights reserved

The moral right of the authors and illustrators has been asserted

Set in Frutiger 55 Roman

Manufactured in China

Except in the United States of America, this book is sold subject to the condition that it shall not,
by way of trade or otherwise, be lent, re-sold, hired out, or otherwise circulated without the publisher's
prior consent in any form of binding or cover other than that in which it is published and without a
similar condition including this condition being imposed on the subsequent purchaser

British Library Cataloguing in Publication Data
A CIP catalogue record for this book is available from the British Library

ISBN 978-0-14056-785-4

This is Sue.

Nick likes red apples.

Sue likes green pears.

Nick likes yellow socks.

Sue likes yellow ducks.

Nick likes orange hair.

Sue likes purple hair...

...and purple flowers.

Nick likes brown bears

and black cats.

Sue likes black and white cats

and black and
white hats.

Nick likes red cars.

Sue likes pink and orange cars.

Nick likes pink and

orange dinosaurs.

Sue likes red rockets

and red dogs.

Nick likes green aliens.

Sue likes green and yellow aliens.

Nick likes green and red

and pink and orange

and yellow and purple jelly.

Sue likes everything blue.

Sue likes Nick.

Nick likes Sue.

Goodbye Nick!
Goodbye Sue!